The Abandoned

Written by Casey Raff

2017

Chapter 1

He had never been inside this house before but it was one he had driven past a time or two each month. It was located along a road that didn't get much traffic as this was a rural part of the area. There wasn't much within the proximity of the house either. Just some trees here and there and some fields with overgrown, yellowed grass and brambles. The occasional beer bottle was found in ditches that lined the old road. Steve wasn't the type of person to be scared about things that might or might not exist in the natural or supernatural world. He didn't possess the sense of anything that could bother him that much. He had gotten an odd feeling a time or two when he drove by this house but nothing that would scare him from wanting to drive by it anymore. In fact, he found a growing fascination of wanting to investigate it; to see what it was like, to see what he could find or not find. He figured that he wasn't the only person that had been in it after it had been abandoned. If there was anything of value or interest that this house might contain, it most likely wouldn't be in there anymore.

Steve walked up the wooden steps that led to the front door. With each step that he took, the steps let out an agonized sound like an old gate that never got oiled. He reached the top of the stairs and looked around the exterior of the house. It wasn't his house; he didn't belong here and neither did anybody else. It was a vacant house that had been that way for some time. The outside was in poor condition and the interior was probably in much the same shape.

He got to the front door and pushed it open. It squeaked on its old, rusty hinges. The smell of dry dirt wafted out and lingered in his sinuses. He took a breath and walked inside. The drywall was cracked and brittle plasterboards were visible in those areas where holes were either caused by somebody who had punched them in or they just occurred naturally with the variant weather conditions year after year. Much of the carpet was just patches of fuzz, like mold on a rotting peach. He could see the old floorboards and wondered if they would hold his weight as he walked over them. He slowly walked around what he imagined was the living room. With each step he could feel the floor bend under his feet, he could barely hear the slight cracking sounds of the wood threatening to break. Since it was late afternoon, there was an adequate amount of light coming in through the west windows. He saw a hallway to the right and walked towards it. There were a couple of entry-ways along the right side of the hall and one on the left side. At the end of the hall was another door that was halfway open. Unlike the other entryways, he couldn't see what was inside of this area. He figured it was maybe a closet since it was so dark but since he was at the opposite end of it, still at the beginning of the hall, he couldn't quite come to that conclusion of it being a closet. He held off on walking down the hall for the time being. He turned and walked into the kitchen. Old cupboards hung from the ceiling and most of the doors were just hanging from one hinge, dangling there like hangnails. Cobwebs were inside all the cupboards and mouse and rat droppings were scattered across the shelves like chocolate, crispy cereal.

Dirt that belonged outside had been tracked inside, probably from previous visitors, along with old pine needles that dropped from the trees as the seasons got colder. The house also had that peculiar dank, musty smell that old cellars usually have. He inched toward the door that was at the end of the dim hall and as he approached the opening, he peered down to get a look. It was just blackness down there. He could barely make out the second step of the staircase that led down. There was an old, rusted tin can lying on the floor in the hall. He picked it up and dropped it into the blackness that was beyond the door. He could hear it as it bounced hollowly down the wooden steps and it let out a dull thud as it hit what he assumed to be the concrete floor of the basement. Other than that, the house remained eerily silent.

It wasn't much longer when he heard muffled, pattering sounds. He turned around and walked down the hall to one of the bedrooms. He could see from the window that the sound he heard was rain that was falling. A slight draft came through the broken window and along with it came the smell of earth caused by the rain. It smelled like decomposing leaves, moss and dirt. Any other time the smell wouldn't have bothered him but now it reminded him of death and all the things that could be around him.

The room grew darker as heavy, grey clouds passed, overtaking the smaller, whiter clouds. He glanced at his watch and saw that it was almost 4:00. Steve walked out of the bedroom and looked around at the living room one last time before deciding to go home. He would come back another time when he was more prepared. Although there was nothing in the house worth coming back to, he felt the urge, the need, to check out the basement.

Chapter 2

The following week, Steve drove back to the house. He had his pair of black, rubber boots and a flashlight next to him on the passenger seat of his truck. He also donned his stocking cap as this day was a little bit colder than the previous week. He also felt more comforted with it on as a child does with a blanket when they are anxious.

He turned off onto the driveway that led to the old house, the wheels of his truck making crunching sounds as he drove over the gravel. He turned his truck off and glanced at his watch. It was a quarter past one. He would have plenty of time to check things out. He got out of his truck and walked towards the house. The air around him seemed stale; it didn't feel right. He stopped and continued looking at the house in front of him. It just stood there in front of him, beckoning to him. He felt a queer sort of jolt rise up through his spine. He started towards the house again and unlike the last time, he walked around the side of the house into the backyard. Here there was dried, yellow grass that went almost up to his knees and there were lots of old, rusted cans and old garbage bags that were in various stages of deteriorating. Large ferns were growing out of an old tree stump and the base of it was lined with dry moss. He walked around the other side of the house back towards the front and stepped over a doll that was halfway buried in the ground in thin, loose soil. He imagined that it belonged to some little girl once upon a time and she and the doll had been the prettiest things in that house. Now as he peered down at the doll, he saw no prettiness, nothing happy about the scene at all. It laid there motionless, its dirt-caked face and open eyes staring into Steve's. He felt the need to break visual contact with the doll so he gave it a swift kick and watched it flail about as one of its legs came off as it bounced along the hard dirt.

He walked up the porch steps as he had done the previous time and was stupidly surprised when he heard a loud crack. His foot went crashing through the rotten step that had given out under his weight. Luckily, he had his rubber boots on as it probably saved his shin from getting too badly damaged; it still hurt none the less but that pain was subsided with endorphins along with his anxious feelings that now came about him. Part of him told himself to just turn around and forget this foolishness, to just go back to his truck and drive home or drive somewhere else; anywhere but here where he had no business being. But he didn't listen to that thought. He pushed it aside much like he did with the front door as he walked through it. He stood in the living room to recollect himself, waiting for his eyes to adjust to the dimness of the house, the musty smell filling his senses. He had already looked around the house and found nothing of interest the week before so he proceeded down the hall towards the basement door. To his surprise, the door was closed. He slowed his steps but his pulse increased. During his first visit here, the door had been halfway open. He told himself to think logically, that a gust of wind had blown hard enough through the broken windows and caused it to close. He told himself that a dozen times but it still didn't make him feel any better. It took him about two minutes to muster up the courage to grasp the doorknob. It was cold. *Of course it would be*, he told himself. He turned it, listening to the latch click and the door made an enormously loud creaking sound as he pulled it open slowly. The slower he pulled it open, the louder it seemed to get. He took a deep breath and sneezed due to the dank, stale air that bellowed up from below.

He turned his flashlight on and saw his first view into what was once darkness. It was just a long, narrow flight of stairs, about fifteen steps in all, walls bordering both sides, and at the bottom of the stairs was another closed door. Resting against the door was the tin can he had tossed down the steps last week. He took his first step down and immediately wondered what he was doing and why he was doing it but was unable to answer any of his questions. There were no handrails going down, at least not anymore if there ever had been any, so he used the walls to steady himself. Halfway down, his hand went through the rotten drywall and plunged into spider webs that were behind it. He reached the bottom finally and paused at the door, hesitant to open it. A few seconds later he raised his hand and knocked softly on the door. *Just what in the hell are you doing knocking on that door?!* He cursed at himself. *There's no one here to answer it. Do you really expect someone to open it and invite you inside?*

He stopped that thought right there but others took its place. *What if all of a sudden the door did open and there stood somebody, something, covered in dirt and all kinds of other nasty things. Or, what if that thing is just waiting for you behind that closed door or waiting for you to open the door and step inside so it can come out of its spot where it was huddled somewhere in a dark corner or perhaps crouched behind a furnace and crawl out or -*

He decided to put his ear close to the door and listened. All he could hear was the sound of his heavy breathing. Other than that, the house was quiet. He pondered just walking back up the stairs and calling the whole thing off but he had made it this far and he was determined to go through with this. He took a breath, found his hand grasping the doorknob and before he knew it he had pushed open the door. Almost immediately, the smell of old oil came into his senses followed by a rotten smell that made him gag. He waved his flashlight around the room. The first thing he saw was an old furnace in one corner of the room; it was covered in cobwebs and was rusty; to his relief, nothing came crawling out from behind it. A few feet from it was an old water heater, equally as rusted as the furnace. There was also a washer and dryer. To his surprise, there was no rust on them but they were dirty. On the opposite side of the room was an old, wooden workbench.

The lid on the washer was open but the dryer was closed and had a latch over it. Affixed to the latch was a tiny lock. He walked over to the washer and cautiously peered inside. He drew his head back in disgust. The washer was filled with some kind of thick, sludgy goop. Its color was that of rotten bile: dark green, almost black. The smell was as close to horrendous as he could imagine; it was like rotten meat mixed in a broth of raw sewage. Although he was disgusted, he was also curious. He looked back in at the contents and found floating globs of brownish chunks. He looked around and found a plunger nearby. He used it to stick into the washer. He could feel that something was stopping the plunger from reaching the depths of the bottom, an almost spongy feeling as he poked into the mess. He slowly pulled it back out an angle to see if he could fish anything out. On his first attempt, he came up with nothing. He tried again and got the same results. His third time, he could feel he was pulling something up but as it reached the surface, it slipped off. Getting annoyed, he gave up and examined the lock on the dryer. It was firmly locked. He looked around to see if there was anything he could use to break it open. Nothing.

He thought to himself that he would come back the following week and bring his toolbox with him. He was curious as to why the dryer was locked and why it was not broke open. Surely someone had to have been down here before. He couldn't have been the only one and if someone had been down here, they wouldn't just leave here without wanting to know why it was locked, just as he kept on wondering. He made up his mind. He would go home now and get his toolbox and come right back. He couldn't wait another week. What if someone else came during that time and made the discovery themselves?

He walked out of the basement closing the door behind him at the bottom of the stairs. He ascended the steps and closed the door at the top of the steps as well. As he walked down the hall, he turned off his flashlight to conserve its battery. He made a mental note to himself to bring his headlamp with him so his hands would be free.

Chapter 3

He skipped dinner when he got home. He didn't have time to cook anything as he just wanted to get back to that house. By the time he got all his tools together, it was already quarter to six; the sun had just set not long ago and twilight was taking over the sky. As he was driving he felt anxious; really anxious. It was an exciting feeling but also a nervous feeling. Back when Steve had been in his twenties, his friends had dared him to go bungee-jumping with them. Steve was reluctant at first but peer-pressure always seems to win. He remembered having that same nervous feeling of excitement as he had now but why was he doing this; there was no peer-pressure this time.

Like he had done earlier that day, Steve pulled into the gravel driveway that led to the house. Only this time, things seemed different, it was an off-settling feeling. For starters, the sound of the crunching that the gravel made as he drove over it seemed more sinister, hollower. As his headlights lit up the house, it loomed there in the openness; like a shadow on a sunless day, it seemed unnatural. He sat in his truck just looking at the house; its windows broken, the siding dirty and rotted, shingles dangling from the eaves of the roof like teeth hanging from their gangly roots; the front porch as crooked as the smile on a kid's jack-o-lantern. Everything about it made it something it wasn't but here Steve was making all that possible with the complexities of his imagination.

He strapped the headlamp onto his head, grabbed his toolbox and got out of the truck. He walked towards the house, the air around him feeling thick with humidity. He could smell stagnant moss and decomposing leaves and that conjured the image of the doll he had kicked earlier. Its lifeless body still laying somewhere around the corner of the house in the dirt. It's eyes open. He shook his head trying to shake the image from his mind. He reached into the side of his coat and produced a bottle. While he was at his house earlier, he had gotten into the cupboard above his fridge and decided to bring a pint of whisky with him. Now he put the bottle to his lips and took three rather large pulls off of it and could instantly feel the liquid burn his throat and warm his body. He put the lid back on and saw he had drunk half of its contents. That was ok though; it seemed necessary to get that liquid courage flowing through his blood as his real courage was not cooperating with him. His thoughts went back to that day of bungee-jumping with his friends, *Good ole whiskey…Good ole peer-pressure.*

Steve let himself into the house and moved his head around to inspect his surroundings with the headlamp. The house seemed a lot smaller in the dark, his headlamp lighting up the interior in small sections. This made it spookier. He wasn't scared of the dark. Steve was never scared of the dark, even as a kid he wasn't. He recalled lying in bed one late night when he was about eight years old. His room was completely dark. After a while, the clouds had drifted to other parts of the sky and exposed the moon which shone in through his window scantly lighting his room up. There on the wall had been a big, brown, hairy spider. He felt his body tense and tighten almost to the point that it was painful. The next morning, he woke up and told his parents about the spider that had been there in the dark and how it had frightened him, that he didn't want to sleep in his room anymore. His parents laughed with amusement and told Steve that if he wouldn't have seen the spider he would have been just fine.

I'm not afraid of the dark, Steve now reminded himself some forty years later. *I'm not afraid of the dark; I'm just afraid of what is IN the dark.* With that thought going through his mind, he turned toward the hallway and walked towards the closed door that led to the basement. His body was sweating despite the coolness of the house. He opened the door and started to descend the stairs when he stopped cold in his tracks. The door at the bottom of the stairs was slightly open. He felt goose bumps start to form up and down his arms. He remembered closing it before he had left. There was no way the wind could have blown it open as the upper door had been closed. Steve thought about calling out but the thought of hearing his own words in this narrow stairwell spooked him. He didn't want to hear his words bounce hollowly off the walls down into the nothingness of the room below. So instead, he continued down, slowly; so slow that it became suspenseful with each step that brought him closer to the door.

As he entered the room, his light caught sight of something leaning up against the corners of the wall on the far side of the basement. Its configuration appeared to be of a body wrapped in a sheet. His mouth felt dry and his limbs went numb. The toolbox fell out of his hand and slammed to the floor with a deafening crash as tools of all sorts of shapes and sizes clanged and clinked as they scattered across the floor. That sound only intensified as it echoed off the walls and then it became eerily silent. Steve didn't know what to do. He almost liked the sound the tools had made because it distracted him. Now the only thing distracting him was this dark, silent house. He stood there like a statue, wanting to move but not being able to. He was unsure of how long he stood there before he finally mustered up the strength to move. He knew for damn sure that he wouldn't be going anywhere near that sheet.

You're not afraid of the dark, you're just afraid of what's in the dark. Steve wondered why he had thought about this but his thoughts continued on. *Here you see a sheet which looks like it contains a body; it is here for you to see. Yet, there is a locked dryer.*

You have no idea what it contains but yet you want to open it. Do you really want to see what is in that dark spot?

This whole house was a dark spot now that he came to think about it. He had entered it not knowing what it might contain and now that he was in here, he was committed. *If I was anymore committed, I would be in the fucking loony-bin right about now but no, here I am. I am that thing in the dark that you never wanted to see. I am that thing waiting down here like a bad nightmare waiting for a kid to fall asleep. I am that body in the sheet. I am the person that put that body in the sheet. I am whatever this house wants me to be. This house is whatever I want it to be. We control each other. It makes me feel fear. I make it seem fearful. It was just as innocent as I was until the two of us came together.* He could feel himself starting to lose his sanity. Little by little this situation was breaking him down, devouring him into small fragments. Each thought was like a jolt of electricity being plunged directly into his nerves and shorting out whatever functioning receptors and neurotransmitters were left of his brain. He imagined that this is what decomposition would feel like once death takes over. The maggots and bacteria breaking everything down until there is nothing left but bone; an internal structure that housed everything you once knew.

He bent down and slowly gathered up his tools, placing them into the toolbox one at a time to minimize noise. His hands were shaking while he did this. After he was done, he glanced around the basement again, the lights bouncing off of the walls and he focused his eyes onto the sheet. He allowed himself to calm down. He took deep breaths and slowly let them out rhythmically until he felt he could fully rationalize the situation, to think things through with a clear mind. *Yes, there is a sheet and it does look bulky but it could be something else and not the body that you are thinking could be in there. Is it possible that you just overlooked it when you were down here before?* Steve thought about these ponderings for a while and concluded that it was very possible, that this could be the case but he also wondered how he could have missed it. It just didn't make sense. *It's not supposed to make sense. You are standing down here in an abandoned house at night and you're trying to make sense of all this. Forget it Steve-baby, just forget it. What you are doing is senseless. Just do what you came here to do and get done with it and get out. Talking to yourself is bad. You are hindering yourself from any progress you could have already made. Just get yourself together and get on with it.*

He stood there another minute and wondered if he should check out the dryer, as he had originally intended or check out the sheet. He decided checking the sheet would be the best option as the dryer was locked. The sheet seemed to pose more of a danger, more of a threat which made Steve wonder if he should just flee up the steps and leave the mysteries of this place. Steve inched his way toward the sheet and reached his hand out. *Don't think about it.* He clutched the sheet with trembling fingers. *Do it!* He pulled on the sheet firmly and ran back fast as whatever was under the sheet was now falling with the sheet. It hit the floor with a muffled thud and remained still. Steve turned his head downward to direct the beam of the light onto the floor. He could see what was in the sheet was what appeared to be just a mannequin. It's face pale and eyes open, seeing nothing. This made him think of the doll outside. Only this time he wasn't going to kick the mannequin as he had done with the doll.

Steve being more relaxed now turned his attention toward the dryer but his nerves were still shot. He set his toolbox down on the floor in front of it and reached into to grab his hack-saw. It took him about five minutes to cut through the lock; although it was small it was strong. He could feel excitement build up in him as he put his hand on the latch, undoing it, then he opened the dryer. He was shocked at what he saw. This situation just kept getting stranger and stranger. The insides of the dryer were completely gone. At the bottom of the dryer was a thick cylinder of cement, the kind you might see in sewage systems. It was in there vertically going through the bottom of the dryer and to Steve's amazement it went into the floor. His heart thudded in his chest. He could smell the wet earth coming up the chamber of the pipe. He debated on leaning into the dryer so that he could see down into the pipe but his gut-instinct told him not to. Anything he was previously feeling from the whisky no longer had any effect on him. He produced the bottle from his jacket and drank the rest of it, regretting not bringing a bigger bottle. Reaching into his tool-box, he got his hammer out with no interest in using it for what it was intended for; for now it would serve purpose as a way of defending himself if needed.

Taking a deep breath, he leaned into the dryer and peered down the cement pipe. He saw there were make-shift rungs made of bent metal bars. The pipe was about seven feet deep and opened to dirt. He could see black garbage bags on the ground; some looked empty, others looked like they had stuff in them. Steve wondered to himself why somebody would take the time to construct all of this. He thought of how to get down there and stupidly found himself facing away from the dryer, laying on the floor on his stomach and slowly crawled backwards like a worm and worked his feet into the opening of the dryer, pushing himself up with his arms and pushing back to get the rest of himself into the dryer as his legs bent at a painful angle into the pipe. His feet found the rungs and he was nearly all the way into the dryer, just his head was poking out of the opening. He climbed down and his feet hit the surface of the dirt which felt like he was standing on a firm sponge. He couldn't believe he was down here. His heart was beating triple-time and he was sweating profusely. The dug-out

chamber was only high enough for him
to stand uncomfortably hunched over.
It was about six feet wide and six feet
long. He gently kicked at one of the
garbage bags and that is when he about
had his first heart attack. A single
decomposing hand came out of the bag
and landed palm up in the dirt. Steve let
out a scream but the sound was
absorbed by the walls of dirt. He had
had enough. His hands found the
bottom rung of the pipe and he pulled
himself up until he was able to climb it
like a ladder.

His head just came out of the
opening of the dryer when Steve had
his near-second heart attack only
minutes apart from his first one. He
barely heard the sound of a door
opening and then closing; seconds later

he could hear foot-steps and the creaking sounds of floorboards being walked upon.

Steve could not move; he just waited there in the dryer and that is when it came to him that his headlamp was still on. He really didn't want to turn it off but he also didn't want to keep it on. It didn't really matter though. Either way, he would be found, headlamp or no headlamp, it was just a matter of time. He had nowhere to go. His only means of escape were up those stairs. He cursed at himself for not getting out of the dryer. He would have had a better chance being out in the openness of the basement. He didn't know what to do and he had only seconds to figure out a plan. There was nothing he could do to conceal the fact that he had been down here and still was; his toolbox was sitting next to the dryer, the cut lock next to it.

Without thinking further, Steve crawled out of the dryer. He heard another door opening; only this sound was louder, it was the door at the top of the stairs. He looked around manically. He reached down and grabbed some zip-ties from his toolbox, placing them in the pocket of his jeans. He ran to the corner of the basement and crouched down before turning off his headlamp.

Faintly, footfalls could be heard coming down the steps, one by one, slowly but purposefully. Steve waited in the darkness, so many thoughts rushing through his head, trying to think of what he would do. That was when he heard the sound of the door at the bottom of the steps creaking open. He waited to see some kind of light because it would be impossible for whoever was coming in to see where they were going but Steve saw no light. A chill went down his spine and back up until he felt the shock hit his head and it was a split moment later when his world went black.

Chapter 4

Steve awoke to someone slapping his face, almost like how a cat would playfully slap a mouse around and he felt a wetness on the side of his head. He tried to reach up to massage his head but found his hands were bound behind his back so he resorted to screaming instead. This only provoked laughter from whoever was doing this to him, putting him through this torture. Oddly, the room was still dark. He flailed about like a fish out of water but saw that it wasn't doing him any good; in fact, it only brought on more pain to his wrists as he guessed it was his own zip-ties that were being used to secure him as the edges dug into his wrists. He heard a familiar, soft striking sound and saw the flame as it appeared on a match which was then used to light a candle that was a couple of feet away from him.

"Why are you doing this?" Steve asked, his voice shaking along with the rest of his body. He looked around the best he could but couldn't see much of anything besides the candle and what appeared to be a set of night-vision goggles.

"Did I tell you to talk?" the voice responded back. It was the voice of a man.

Steve didn't know how to answer or if he should answer so he didn't.

The unknown man shot into view in front of Steve and before Steve could react, he felt a sharp pain wash across his face as the man slapped him. It made a sound like a tree branch snapping. His face burned with madness along with the physical pain.

"Now let me ask you again, did I tell you to talk?"

"No" Steve said trembling.

"Then why are you talking?" The man's hand lashed out again and Steve, preparing himself for a slap, wasn't prepared for the punch that came instead. The hit landed firmly on the side of his head, halfway up his ear and he felt it burn as it tingled, his ear ringing.

"What are you doing here?" he asked Steve, pulling his tool chest across the ground and propping himself on it about a foot away from where Steve laid on the ground. Steve saw that the man was wearing blue, rubber gloves.

Steve didn't answer. He didn't want to anymore. He thought about how to go about his predicament knowing that if he talked he would most likely get hit and if he didn't talk, he would most likely get hit. *Damned if I do and damned if I don't.*

"I see I have frightened you now and we have just met, my friend" the man said grinning. Now that Steve was more aware of his surroundings, he found the man spoke with a deep English accent and he appeared to be in his fifties with shaggy hair and a round belly.

"Allow me to introduce myself if I may; my name is Edgar. I sense you are hating me right now and I can guess why." Edgar spoke firmly but softly, still grinning. "I hate you right now too but we can try to be friends, I suppose, if we just try to understand each other, shall we?

Steve replied with a nod of his head.

"My friend. You must please speak if we are to make sense of all this." Edgar cocked his head sideways to look at Steve who was still lying on his side on the floor. "You poor thing. Let me help you up. You look like a beaten dog down there though I suppose you do feel like one." He laughed at his own analogy as if it was the joke of the day, spittle flying from his mouth onto Steve's face. There was a faint smell of what reminded Steve as spoiled anchovies or oysters. He reached down and pulled Steve up by his shirt so that he was sitting upright.

"Your name please?" Edgar asked Steve. "You may talk. I am done hurting you now"

Steve decided to answer the man this time. "Just quit hitting me, ok? My name is Roy Esthen."

Edgar's grin that he had been grinning for some time now turned flat and then his face scrunched up. He stood up and opened the toolbox and took out a rubber mallet, holding it in front of Steve's face and bringing it down on his kneecap with great force. Steve's leg jerked upward, his foot striking Edgar in the face.

Oh fuck! Steve thought. *I didn't mean that! It was my fucking reflexes. I am going to pay dearly for this one, I know it!*

Edgar sat there, staring at Steve. "I told you we could try to be friends, I tried to be your friend but friends don't lie to each other, no? You lied to me, Steve. You lied. You think I am stupid, no? You are the stupid one my friend. You think I can trust you now that you lied about who you are? It was really simple to be honest but I guess you don't like simple so now we have to play tough." He reached into his pocket and produced Steve's wallet and pulled out his license. "This is your picture, no? This is your name, no? Steve? Huh? **Huh**? You think because I am from different country that you can try and give me false name and I wouldn't find out."

"Well…..Well fuck you!" Steve shouted at him. He didn't care if Edgar *(if that is his real name)* hurt him anymore. *He's right. I am the stupid one. It was stupid of me to come into this house.*

"No…Fuck you, my friend. I know you know what is down here. The washer. The garbage bags. Huh? You stupid, little foolish people. You can't just leave things alone. Perhaps I can add you to my collection. In fact, you leave me no choice for you know what is down here and you have seen me. Or perhaps I can play some more games, huh? Do you like games Steve?" Edgar was getting off on this "I like games Steve! I love games! If you only knew the games I played after I knocked you out! I can kill you now just like I could have hours ago but let's play, huh?"

Hours ago? Steve was confused and scared now. *Hours ago? Have I really been out for hours?* He wondered what time it was.

"What are you talking about? What games?" Steve felt sick to his stomach thinking about the unknown. "What did you do to me?"

Edgar just laughed it off as if it were a stupid question being asked by some annoying kid. "If only you knew. This is just the start. You have no idea how I am about to mess up your life and how I already have."

Steve looked at him with hate. "I'll kill you, you bastard!"

"Try me." Edgar responded with a smug smile.

Steve flung himself backwards as far as he could and landed on his back. Edgar looked at him curiously, got off the toolbox and took a couple of steps towards him and reached down to pick him up. As he did so, Steve used all his force and kicked him square in the chest, sending Edgar backwards. He heard what sounded like a watermelon being dropped onto the ground and raised his head up to see that Edgar's head had struck his toolbox.

Edgar didn't move. He just lay there motionless.

I'm not sure if this is part of the game or not but I gotta act fast! Steve's thoughts raced around and an idea came to him almost at once. *Gotta free my hands up and I think I know how.* He looked at the candle and knew this was his only chance.

Chapter 5

He scooted himself across the floor with his feet. He looked at Edgar. His eyes were closed and blood oozed from his nose and a stream of blood also trickled from the corner of his mouth. Steve contemplated on kicking him hard in the face a couple of times with the bottom of his foot but reconsidered. *I might knock him back to consciousness if I do so. I'm just going to take my chances with how things are. I can't defend myself with my hands bound behind me. I need my hands, dammit!*

Steve eyed the candle again and took a deep breath. *Steady, Steve baby, Steady,* he said to himself as he slowly inched back towards the candle. *Get ready for some pain because there will be plenty of it. There's no way you are getting this on your first try.*

He slowly raised his bound hands behind his back and moved his arms around gently until he felt warmness. He slowly moved his arms back down, feeling the warmness turn into heat as his hands were inches above the flame. Ever so slowly his hands moved around and he felt they found the flame.

Searing pain rushed through his nerves as his flesh was being roasted by the flame. He could smell the sickly scent of burnt hair and skin being wafted around him. He screamed loudly as the pain intensified. He wished he knew exactly how close the zip-ties were to the flame. He just wanted to burn through these damn things and free his hands from not only being bound but also free from the excruciating pain he was bringing on to himself.

Steve wasn't sure how much more he could take. He was close to giving up. He continued moving his hands slowly around and then a nauseating smell hit him and he found he could muster up some form of a smile. The smell was that of burning plastic and he held his hand steady allowing the flame enough time to melt through the zip-tie all the way. He held his breath and closed his eyes tightly. There was still much more pain than he imagined there would be. He was hoping the endorphins would kick in and subdue some of the pain but they didn't.

At last, he felt the zip-tie loosen on his right hand and he was able to bring his hands around in front of him. He opened the tool-chest and found his scissors. As he was cutting off the other zip-tie from his hand, he noticed movement out of the corner of his eye. *Shit! Edgar! I nearly forgot all about him!*

He glanced over at Edgar and saw he was starting to move about. Steve didn't hesitate at all and he picked up the tool chest the best he could with his burnt hands and slammed it down on Edgar's head over and over again. He wasn't sure if it was the sounds of the tools or if it was Edgar's skull being pulverized into fragments but he didn't care. He tuned it out the best he could.

When he was certain that Edgar was unconscious again, Steve found his flashlight laying on the floor and ran to it. He was thankful to see that it still worked. He shone it around the room and was horrified to see fresh blood that he hadn't seen before on the floor. There was an ax laying against the washer and various items scattered about as well.

Steve had lost all interest in this house and whatever was in it. He just wanted to get out of here. He rushed towards the door that led to the stairs leading up and out of the house. Ascending the stairs, he could feel his adrenaline kicking in and the pain in his hands was something he was no longer thinking about. His thoughts raced towards being free as he saw the front door becoming more near with each step he ran.

Chapter 6

Once he was outside, he could faintly see his truck. He got into it (he had left unlocked before he went into the house earlier) reached into his pocket for his keys and found they were not in there.

"Shit!" Steve yelled as he looked towards the house.

There was no way he was going back in there. He had seen enough horror movies to know that you never go back inside of a house once you are out of it.

He jumped out of his truck and made his way towards the road. Steve knew this wasn't the wisest decision either but he felt it was the best one. After running for about five minutes, he heard the sound of a revving engine off in the distance behind him and then he heard tires squealing. Without hesitating, Steve ran off the road and into the thicket of trees until he felt he wouldn't be seen. A couple of minutes later he saw a car slowly driving down the road. To his alarm there was a bright spotlight scanning both sides of the road and that is when he saw the rack of lights on top and knew it was a cop car.

Steve went running towards it, waving his hands and shouting. The car slowed to a stop and a cop jumped out with his gun drawn.

"Put your hands up and get on the ground." The voice of the cop demanded.

"But I need hel-" Steve tried explaining but was cut off by the cop.

"GET ON THE GROUND NOW"

Steve did as he was told being mindful of his burned hands as he tried getting down.

The cop approached him and Steve felt cold metal on his wrists as handcuffs were placed on him and then he was pulled up.

"Please! There's a man! Back there!" Steve said panting "The house!

The abandoned house! He tried to kill me! Oh God, please help!"

"10-4 suspect in custody" the cop said into his radio that was attached to the shirt on his shoulder.

Suspect? Steve thought to himself and then he asked the cop. "Suspect? Of what?"

"You have the right to remain silent. Anything you say or do can be used against you in the court of law. You have the right to an attorney. If you cannot afford an attorney, one will be presented to you by the court of law. Do you understand these rights I have given you?"

"Can you please tell me what this is all about?" Steve pleaded

"Do you understand your rights I have read you?" The cop asked firmly again. "Yes or no?"

Steve's thoughts went back to Edgar and how he had been slapped and punched for not answering questions so he decided it would be wise to start cooperating.

"I guess. Yes." Steve replied. "Now please tell me what this is about."

Suddenly, he saw headlights coming right at him and the cop. The cop pushed Steve out of the way and Steve went tumbling into a ditch, his face getting slammed into the gravel and dirt as he couldn't catch himself with the handcuffs on his wrists. He heard the yell of the cop but couldn't see what had happened.

There was the sound of a car door opening and he heard footsteps coming towards him. Steve felt like he was back in the house again as he couldn't see anything in the darkness and his hands were bound behind his back again; this time with handcuffs instead of zip-ties.

He felt pain as his head was yanked up by his hair and he felt even more pain as he guessed what might have been dry dirt being rubbed onto his face and into his eyes. Steve screamed with pain and regretted it as his mouth was now being filled up with dirt and rocks by whoever was doing this to him. He tossed and kicked about only to feel his ribs being kicked over and over. He was in absolute fear now. Whoever was doing this to him now picked him up and threw him into a car and then they drove off seconds later. Steve could not see anything through his dirt-caked eyes and wondered if he ever would again.

Chapter 7

Ten minutes later, they came to a stop
somewhere and Steve felt himself
being pulled out of the car and thrown
onto the ground. He heard what
sounded like a hose being turned on
and could feel the water as it was being
sprayed onto his upturned face. Then
he was rolled back onto his stomach
and felt excruciating pain as his wrists
were grabbed and he heard a clicking
sound and felt his hands fall limply to

both sides of his body and then he heard the muffled sounds of running footfalls into the distance.

What the hell!? Steve was shaken up. He had no idea what was going on now. He felt like he wasn't even the same person anymore. His nerves were pretty much shot both physically but mainly psychologically. His body shook and shook and he couldn't get it to quit. The harder he tried to stop it from shaking, the more it continued to do so.

He raised his head up off of the cool, wet grass and used his now free hands to wipe at his face. He could still hear the hose running and felt around until he could find it. Once he did, he let the water stream down his face and then tilted his head up and soaked his eyes the best he could. They felt like they had been rubbed with sand-paper but he was thankful that his vision was starting to slightly come back. He was stupidly surprised to see that he was in his own yard.

Disoriented, he got up and walked crookedly towards his house feeling very much like a drunk vagrant you would see down on main street in the city. He got to the front door and reached in his pocket forgetting that he no longer had his keys. Walking around to the side of his house, he clumsily found his spare key that was hung on a branch in a rose bush. It's thorns had found his singed hands a couple of time but Steve didn't care anymore at this point. It didn't even really phase him. He was now used to pain.

He unlocked his door and shut it behind him and locked it. He didn't know whether to call the police as the last he had heard he was a suspect and he wasn't quite sure what they suspected him of. Knowing that he wasn't guilty of anything, he thought it would be best to call and report what had happened so far. He picked up the phone and discovered there was no dial-tone. It was at this moment when he heard the foot-steps coming up behind him and he didn't even have to turn around to know that this was part of the game as he heard a familiar voice.

"Hello, my friend."

Chapter 8

Steve slowly turned around. There was no fear left in him and there was also no fight left in him as well. Here was a game with rules he did not know. A game where he didn't even know what the goal was supposed to be. A game that was just made up by some nut-job. But it was also life and life was not a game.

"I left your wallet back in the house, along with your fingerprints which you had already helped me spread before I had got to you." Edgar stood before him smiling."

Steve felt his body go numb. Edgar was right. It didn't even dawn on him to wear gloves when he went in to look around the house. His prints would be all over; the door knobs, the dryer, the lock that was on the dryer, the rungs of the ladder going down into the ground; Everything would lead back to him. The garbage bag full of body parts and possibly the washer might have body parts in it. His thoughts went back to Edgar in the house. How Edgar had been wearing gloves. Steve saw how this game was being played out now.

"Would you like to hear more" Edgar asked as blood trickled down his badly damaged head from where Steve had struck him with the tool chest. He didn't wait for Steve to give an answer. "I had your keys which you probably already knew. It's a good thing the cop pushed you out of the way as your truck came flying at the two of you. Too bad he couldn't get out of the way fast enough though. It will look like you hit him pretty good as I left your truck there and brought you back here in his car. There will be no record of them ever talking to you. They had no idea who you were at that point. They just knew they had a suspect." Edgar looked out the window and Steve did too. There in the middle of the yard was the cop car that Edgar had stolen and brought Steve back in. Edgar grinned back at Steve. "You do know they will be here soon. Thank you for allowing me to play this game but I am afraid it is now the end of it. I win and you lose." Edgar said walking to the back door as red and blue lights flashed, bouncing off the trees, as cop cars came up the long and winding driveway. He gave Steve one last look as he opened the back door. "Bye, my friend."

Made in United States
Troutdale, OR
07/06/2024